Gala

Red Delicious

Golden Delicious

Macoun

For Emma, who has a star inside —M.M.
For Elaine and Elizabeth and their Bright Red Bookshelf —G.B.K.

The author and the artist wish to thank Willis Wood of Wood's Cider Mill, Springfield, Vermont, and the people of Soons Orchards of New Hampton, New York, particularly Mr. Alan K. Lewis, our orchard guide, for their help researching this story.

Library of Congress Cataloging-in-Publication Data
McNamara, Margaret.
The apple orchard riddle / Margaret McNamara ; pictures by G. Brian Karas.—1st ed.
p. cm.
Summary: When students in Mr. Tiffin's class are invited to solve a riddle during a field trip to an apple orchard, it is Tara's daydreams that may lead to the answer.
ISBN 978-0-375-84744-8 (trade) — ISBN 978-0-375-95744-4 (glb)
[1. Apples—Fiction. 2. School field trips—Fiction. 3. Riddles—Fiction.] I. Karas, G. Brian, ill. II. Title.
PZ7.M47879343App   2013 [E]—dc22   2011008742

The text of this book is set in Century Schoolbook.
The illustrations are rendered in gouache, acrylic, and pencil on paper.
Book design by Rachael Cole

MANUFACTURED IN CHINA
1 3 5 7 9 10 8 6 4 2
First Edition

The Apple Orchard Riddle

By Margaret McNamara • Illustrated by G. Brian Karas

schwartz & wade books · new york

The kids in Mr. Tiffin's class were going on a field trip. "Hurry up, Tara," said Robert. "You'll miss the bus."

Tara took a seat by herself next to the window.
She liked to look outside and wonder about things.

"Tara's in dreamland again," said Anna.

"The lights are on, but nobody's home,"
said Elinor.

Tara didn't hear them. She was
too busy daydreaming.

When they got to the apple orchard, everybody hurried off the bus. Everybody except Tara. Tara walked off slowly. "It takes me a little more time to do things," she said.

"Yes, I've noticed," said Mr. Tiffin.

Hill's
Orchards

come on in!

The class gathered around the orchard's owner, Farmer Hills. "Today," she said, "we are going to take a tour of the orchard. We'll see how apples are picked and how cider is pressed. We'll watch apples get peeled by a special machine. And we'll pick some apples off the trees."

"Plus, I have a riddle for you to solve," said Mr. Tiffin.

"What's the riddle?" asked Charlie.

Mr. Tiffin said, "Show me a little red house with no windows and no door, but with a star inside."

"That's it?" said Jake. "That's the riddle?"

"That's the riddle," said Mr. Tiffin. "Your job is to find the answer."

"How are we going to have time to figure this out while we also have to learn about apples?" asked Molly. "Are you sure this is fair?"

"Yes, I'm sure," said Mr. Tiffin.

"I'm not very good at tests," Tara said.

"That's lucky, because this is not a test," said Mr. Tiffin.

The class walked along a path lined with trees
stretching away as far as they could see.

"We grow twenty varieties of apples here,"
Farmer Hills said. "Who can name some apple varieties?"

"Um . . . McIntosh?" said Alex.

"Granny Smith," said Jeremy.

"Crispin, Fuji, Gala, Red Delicious, Golden Delicious, Macoun!"

"Thank you, Elinor," said Mr. Tiffin.

"Our varieties ripen at different times, so we pick them from late
summer to early fall," said Farmer Hills. "These pointy ladders are
what we use to pick the apples off the highest branches."

"I'm so tall I probably wouldn't need a ladder," said Robert.

"Probably not," said Farmer Hills.

"These branches are so low we can all reach," said Charlie.

"That's right," said Farmer Hills. "Only pick apples off the trees, not off the ground," she added. "To pick an apple, twist the stem till the fruit comes off the branch." She showed the class how to do it and gave them each a small bag for holding apples. They twisted and picked till their bags were full.

Tara didn't pick any apples. Instead, she sat under a tree and looked at the sky. "What was that riddle again?" she asked.

"Show me a little red house with no windows and no door, but with a star inside," said Elinor, who *was* good at tests.

There was an apple on the branch right above Tara's head. Tara twisted it off. "This is red," she said.

Farmer Hills showed the class where the apples were stored. "We keep the apples cold and fresh in this storage barn," she said. "That way, folks can enjoy them all year round."

Jake noticed something about the building.

"A red house!" said Jake. "And look—no windows!"

"But it has two doors," said Anna.

"And Farmer Hills just said it had apples inside, not stars," said Elinor.

"So this is not the answer to the riddle?" said Jake.

"Correct," said Elinor.

Tara wasn't looking at the barn. She was looking at her apple. She saw a tiny worm burrowing into it. "Hey! Look who lives here!" she said.

"Yuck! Don't eat that one," said Robert.

"I won't," said Tara. She laid the wormy apple carefully on the ground. Mr. Tiffin tossed her an apple out of his bag and she took a bite.

At the cider press, Farmer Hills put on a raincoat and hat before she got close to the machine. "Making cider must be a messy business," said Mr. Tiffin.

"And noisy, too," said Farmer Hills.

The class watched as freshly washed apples traveled up a chute to get chopped up into tiny pieces. "This is called pulp," said Farmer Hills.

"Pulp," said Elinor. "Nice word."

Next, a farmhand used a hose to spray the pulp onto canvas sheets.
"Cool!" said Jeremy.
Finally, the sheets of pulp were pressed down hard.
"The juice flows through these sheets into a hose," said Farmer Hills.
"Then it gets pumped into a big metal tank for one last treatment."
"And then it's cider?" asked Charlie.
"Then it's sterilized. And *then* it's cider," said Farmer Hills.

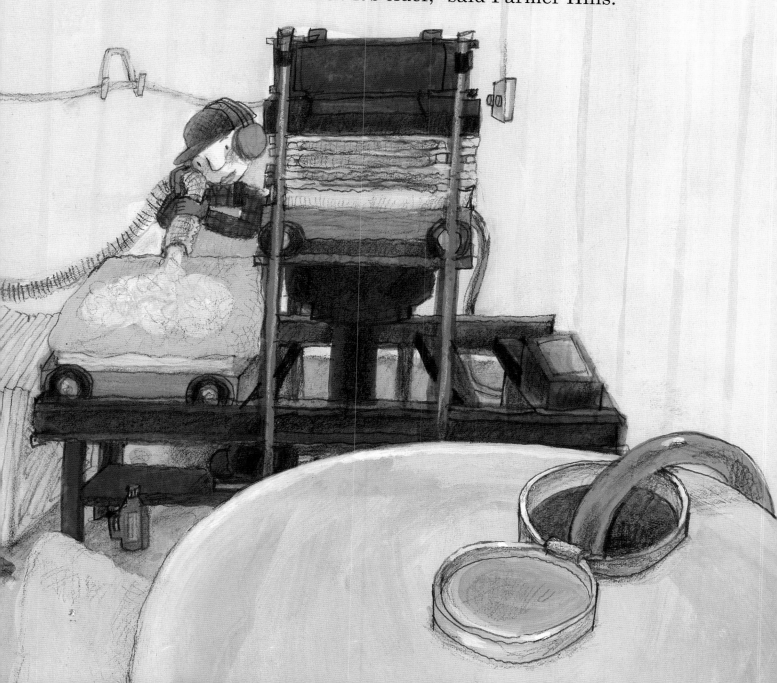

Robert spotted an old tractor as they walked across the farmyard. The tractor was red with rust. "Hey!" he called. "This tractor doesn't have a window or a door!"

Alex and Charlie ran over.

"That's because this is a tractor, not a house," said Alex.

"It could be a house . . . for mice," said Charlie. "Mice sometimes live in a tractor's seat."

Alex and Charlie and Robert poked around the seat.
There were no mice.

"Maybe there's a star inside," said Alex.

Robert and Charlie looked all over the tractor. It had
a steering wheel and a gas gauge and a couple of pedals.

"But no star," said Charlie.

The apple peeler was the next stop. "We use the peeled apples for pies and cakes," said Farmer Hills. She turned the machine on. It peeled each apple in the blink of an eye.

"Whoa!" said Jeremy. "That's fast! Do it again!"

Molly and Kimmy peered into the machine, but they did not get too close.

"It's sort of red," said Kimmy. "Even though it's also a little silver."

"And there are definitely no windows," said Molly.

"No door, either," said Jeremy. "So we win!"

"Yeah, but where's the star?" Kimmy asked.

The three of them watched as the machine peeled the apples one after another.

"No star here," said Kimmy.

At the end of the tour Farmer Hills took the class to the farm stand. "Help yourselves to a cup of apple cider and a cider doughnut," she said.

"Just one each," said Mr. Tiffin.

"But Tara's not eating hers," said Jake.

Tara was still munching on the core of her apple.

"Aren't you done with that yet?" said Robert.

"Not yet," said Tara.

She chewed every last bit of it, till she got to the seeds.
"Five seeds," she said.

Just then, Mr. Tiffin looked at his watch. "Hey, class!" he called. "The bus will be here soon. Let's talk about what we learned today."

"We learned that apples come in a lot of different varieties," said Molly.

"Crispin, Fuji, Gala, Red Delicious, Golden Delicious, Macoun!" said Elinor.

"Cider presses make a lot of noise," said Jeremy.
"Doughnuts are yummy," said Jake.
"How about the riddle?" said Mr. Tiffin.
"There doesn't seem to be an answer," said Elinor.
"I told you it was no fair," said Molly.

Tara walked over to Mr. Tiffin. She had five apple seeds in one hand and a round red apple in another. She handed Mr. Tiffin the apple.

"This is a little red house with no windows and no door," said Tara.

"That's not a house!" said Jake.

"It is if you're a worm," said Tara.

Mr. Tiffin smiled at Tara. "Go on," he said.

"I think there's a star inside this apple," said Tara, "where nobody can see it."

"If nobody can see it, who cares?" said Robert.

"I care," said Mr. Tiffin. "Let's take a look."

The class gathered round. Mr. Tiffin took the apple out of Tara's hand. "Where's the hidden star?" he asked.

"You'll see it if you cut it this way, right across the middle," said Tara.

Mr. Tiffin borrowed a small knife from Farmer Hills. He cut the apple in half, right across the middle.

When he pulled the apple apart, the class could see its five-pointed star. "Hey, Tara was right!" said Molly.

Just then, the bus rumbled down the lane. "Let's give a cheer for Farmer Hills, class," said Mr. Tiffin, and they did.

"The doughnuts were great!" Jake shouted.

The class grabbed their jackets and bags and ran to go home.

"Come on, Tara!" said Mr. Tiffin.

When she got to the bus, Tara chose a seat by herself. She took a bite of an apple with a star inside. Then she looked out the window so she could daydream a little more.

Tara's Apple Orchard
Facts

Orchards are pretty places because there are so many trees.

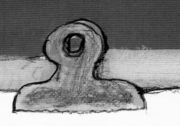

MR. TIFFIN'S APPLE ORCHARD FACTS

- Apple farmers plant different varieties of trees in their orchards. The apples ripen at different times so that they can be harvested in batches, not all at once. At Hills Orchard, the first apples to become ripe are McIntosh and Gala in late summer, followed by Red Delicious, Golden Delicious, Crispin, and Macoun in early fall. Fuji and Granny Smith are the last to be harvested, right up to the last week of November.

- At almost all orchards, each apple is picked by hand. Apple pickers wear a picking bucket with a special canvas bottom that holds the apples while the picker is up a ladder. When the bucket is full, the apple picker carefully pulls a string on either side of the bucket and the apples are released into a large bin.

- The picked apples are washed by machine and sorted by farm workers. The prettiest apples are sold at farmers' markets and grocery stores. Apples that are not so good-looking are sold to companies that make food containing apples—applesauce or apple turnovers, for instance. One secret a farmer knows is that an apple does not have to look perfect to taste perfect. Now you know, too.

- Farmer Hills's apple cooler preserves apples at a temperature of 33° F, just above freezing. This can keep them fresh-tasting for up to eight months.

- Many apple farms have cider presses like the one on Farmer Hills's farm. Apple cider contains apple pulp, so it's darker than apple juice, which is filtered and clear.

- It takes under two seconds for the apple peeler on Farmer Hills's farm to peel a whole apple!

- Every apple hides a star. Ask a grown-up the same riddle I asked my class. If they can't think of the answer (and I bet they won't be able to), bring them an apple and ask them to cut it carefully around the middle, or the equator. Then surprise them with the star inside.

McIntosh

Granny
Smith

Crispin

Fuji